STARS OF SPORTS

CHLOE KIM

GOLD-MEDAL SNOWBOARDER

■■❚❚ by *Matt Chandler*

CAPSTONE PRESS
a capstone imprint

Stars of Sports is published by
Capstone Press, an imprint of Capstone
1710 Roe Crest Drive, North Mankato, Minnesota 56003
www.capstonepub.com

**Library of Congress Cataloging-in-Publication Data is available on the Library
of Congress website.**
ISBN: 978-1-5435-9174-3 (hardcover)
ISBN: 978-1-5435-9187-3 (eBook PDF)

Summary: At 17 years old, Chloe Kim became the youngest woman to win an
Olympic snowboarding medal. She was the first snowboarder to win half-pipe gold
at the Olympics, the World Championships, and the X Games. This bio covers all of
her achievements and more.

Editorial Credits
Christianne Jones, editor; Ashlee Suker, designer; Eric Gohl, media researcher;
Laura Manthe, production specialist

Image Credits
Alamy: Action Plus Sports Images, 15; Associated Press: Alex Goodlett, 28, Invision/
Phil McCarten, 23, Julie Jacobson, 11, Summit Daily News/Hugh Carey, 24–25;
Newscom: AFLO/Hiroyuki Sato, 12, 13, Kyodo, 19, Reuters/Dylan Martinez, 5,
Reuters/Mike Blake, cover, 6 (front), YNA/Yonhap News, 16; Shutterstock: Alex Tor,
8, Angel La Canfora, 6 (back), Kathy Hutchins, 20, PradaBrown, 9, SoisudaS, 27,
Tinseltown, 22, TSLPhoto, 1

Printed in the United States of America.
PA99

FEBRUARY 2020

TABLE OF CONTENTS

Glossary terms are **BOLD** on first use.

GOLDEN GIRL

Snowboarder Chloe Kim stood at the top of the hill ready to make history. Kim was competing in her first Olympics. The 17-year-old checked her goggles. She adjusted her mittens. With a deep breath she launched herself down the hill.

Kim shot high into the air, completing a **1080-degree flip** and landing perfectly. She immediately climbed the **half-pipe** and landed another perfect 1080. Kim slid to the bottom of the mountain. She had just won the Olympic gold medal in half-pipe!

Her amazing run at the 2018 Winter Olympics earned her a spot in the record books. The American teenager became the youngest woman to win an Olympic medal in snowboarding.

Kim soars above the half-pipe at the 2018 Winter Olympics. 〉〉〉

CHAPTER ONE

CALIFORNIA SNOWBOARDER

California isn't full of snow. But that hasn't stopped Kim! She was born in Long Beach, California. She was raised in nearby Torrance. Kim has become one of the most successful female snowboarders in history.

Her dad showed her the sport when she was 4 years old. Two years later, Kim entered her first competition. She won junior nationals the next year. Her dad knew his daughter had a gift. He quit his job to travel with Kim and help her focus on snowboarding.

⟨⟨⟨ Kim celebrates her Olympic gold medal with her mom.

TEEN TALENT

Kim left California when she was in third grade. She was only 8 years old. Her parents sent her to live with her aunt in Switzerland. Her dad wanted her to learn French and go to school there.

She continued her snowboard training in the European mountains. Her mom and dad would visit her in Switzerland. Her dad would take her to the **Swiss Alps** to practice.

⟩⟩⟩ Ski slopes in the Swiss Alps

>>> Mammoth Mountain, California

The hours of training and hard work paid off. Kim entered the Burton European Open Junior Jam in Switzerland in 2010. This event is for the world's top half-pipe riders under 14. Kim won first place. She was only 9 years old!

Kim returned to the United States in 2010. She began training at Mammoth Mountain in California. She spent most of her time on the mountain. She didn't even get to go to school with her friends. Instead, she was homeschooled through an online program.

FACT

Kim speaks three languages—English, French, and Korean.

CHAPTER TWO
YOUNG STAR

By the time she was 13, Kim had become one of the most exciting snowboarders to watch. She was a natural. She was so good that she made the 2014 Winter Olympics team.

However, snowboarders must be at least 15 to compete in the Olympics. So Kim didn't get to travel to Russia. Instead, she watched the Olympic games from her couch with a bowl of ice cream. She would have to wait two more years for her shot at Olympic glory.

Kim watched the replay of her second run 〉〉〉 at the 2013 Dew Tour Championship.

>>> Kim sails to big heights at the 2014 Winter X Games.

X GAMES CHAMPION

Kim was too young for the 2014 Olympics. But she kept busy. She went to her first Winter X Games in 2014 in Aspen, Colorado. She competed against American Kelly Clark. Clark was considered the greatest women's snowboarder in history.

Kim made a strong showing in the **superpipe** event. In her final run, Kim reached 13 feet 9 inches (3.96 meters) above the pipe in one of her jumps. The judges were impressed. Kim scored 94.33 (out of 100) on her final run. Kim was in third place going into the last run.

Clark took home the gold medal. But Kim's awesome final run earned her a silver medal. It was her first X Games medal. Over the next five years, she won five gold medals and a bronze at the X Games.

〉〉〉 Kim (left) on the medal stand with Kelly Clark (middle) and Kaitlyn Farrington (right).

CHAPTER THREE

YOUTH OLYMPIAN

Kim's first Olympic games came in 2016. Kim was part of the U.S. team at the 2016 Winter Youth Olympics in Norway. She competed against the most talented snowboarders in the world.

In the half-pipe she delivered three solid runs. She beat 15 others for the gold medal. Her final run earned her a score of 96.5 from the judges.

Many people were surprised when Kim earned a second medal. With her focus on the half-pipe, Kim had not practiced the **slope style** event much. Her 88.25 score easily topped the second place score of 82.25. She took home her second gold of the week.

Fighting Spirit

In 2016, Kim was part of the United States team that traveled to Norway for the Winter Youth Olympic Games. The 15-year-old star was sick and hurt at the games. But she never gave up and won two gold medals!

‹‹‹ Kim competed at the 2016 Red Bull X Games in Oslo, Norway.

>>> In 2017, Kim tested her skills at the FIS World Cup in PyeongChang, South Korea.

It takes hard work to compete at the Olympic level. So what was it like for Kim to prepare herself for a chance at the 2018 Olympics? For starters, it took thousands of hours of practice.

Kim worked out as many as six hours a day. A normal day for the teen included at least three hours of nonstop practice on the half-pipe. Kim would ride more in the afternoon.

Then she would watch film of her practice with her coach. One small turn or one missed hand grab of the board could cost a rider a gold medal. Kim watched film to get better and get rid of those small mistakes.

STRIKING GOLD

After years of waiting, it was time. Kim finally had her chance to represent the United States at the Winter Olympics. The 2018 Games were extra special for the 17-year-old. Her parents **emigrated** from South Korea in 1982. The 2018 games were held in PyeongChang, South Korea. Her whole family was there.

Winning a medal in her first Olympics wouldn't be easy. Kim was one of 24 **competitors** in the women's half-pipe event. Only the top 12 would make it to the finals.

The United States had four women competing in the half-pipe event. All four reached the finals, including Kelly Clark. Clark held three Olympic medals in the half-pipe competition.

But Kim was unstoppable. She was the best and easily took home her first gold medal. Her winning score of 98.25 was 8.5 points ahead of second place.

Never Let Up

The gold medal was hers. She didn't need to do anything special in her final run. But that isn't how Chloe Kim thinks. Instead of playing it safe, she made a historic final run. Kim landed two 1080s in a row.

Kim attended the 2018 Billboard Music Awards in Las Vegas.

CHAPTER FOUR

AFTER THE OLYMPICS

Before she won an Olympic gold medal, Kim was famous in the world of snowboarding. After she took home an Olympic medal, she was famous worldwide. Kim appeared on TV. She posed for the cover of Sports Illustrated. She was on a box of Corn Flakes.

Kim has said that her new fame can be tough. She is recognized everywhere she goes. She can't just go to a restaurant to eat or walk down the street. Fans want to pose for selfies with her. Others want an autograph.

Kim also wants to help others. As a Korean-American, Kim says she knows how it feels to be bullied. She hopes to help young people speak out against bullying.

FACT

Kellogg's Corn Flakes has been putting athletes on its cereal boxes for decades. Kim's box in 2018 was the fastest selling in Corn Flakes history.

SOCIAL SNOWBOARDER

Sports fans know Kim as a top snowboarder. But she has even more fans on **social media**. She has a huge following on Twitter and Instagram.

In the middle of her Olympic competition, she sent a tweet that instantly went **viral**. Between half-pipe runs, she tweeted about being "hangry."

〉〉〉 Kim was all smiles at the Nickelodeon's Kids' Choice Awards in 2018.

CHLOE KIM
BEST FEMALE ATHLETE

〉〉〉 The award for best female athlete at the 2018 ESPY Awards went to Kim.

Kim uses her social media to connect with fans. On a snowboard, she is an Olympic champion. But on social media, she is just another teenager. She tweets about her favorite foods and shopping.

Ice Cream Please

Kim captured the attention of the world by tweeting about her love of ice cream at the 2018 Olympics. She even carried a dish of it with her to snack on during interviews. Kim's love of ice cream was a huge news story at the Olympics.

23

GOLDEN COMPETITOR

After winning Olympic gold, Kim was a celebrity. There were interviews. There were commercials. There were parties. But if she was going to return to the Olympics in four years, Kim had to get back to training.

Kim returned to **international** competition almost 10 months after the Olympics. Would she be out of practice? Would her new duties get in the way of her job on the snow? Fans soon found out the answers to those questions.

Kim flies through the air at the Toyota U.S. Grand Prix event in 2018.

In December 2018, Kim headed to Colorado for the 2018 World Cup half-pipe event. Kim delivered a 92.25 on her second run. That was more than enough to win the event. Kim was still golden!

CHAPTER FIVE

OFF THE SLOPES

Kim has made history in the snowboarding world. She is also successful off the snow. She has starred in TV commercials. She has modeled for magazines. Her face is on many products. Thanks to snowboarding, Kim will earn millions of dollars. But most of that money will come without a snowboard strapped to her feet.

Kim is ready to continue her studies. She was accepted to Princeton University. She wants to study science. She is interested in many careers. No matter what she picks, Kim has her sights set on changing the world when her snowboarding career is over.

Unstoppable

At the 2019 U.S. Open, Kim was the defending champion. After an opening-round run on the half-pipe, Kim took off her board and limped along the course. She completed two more runs and earned a silver medal. X-rays later showed she broke her ankle on the first run.

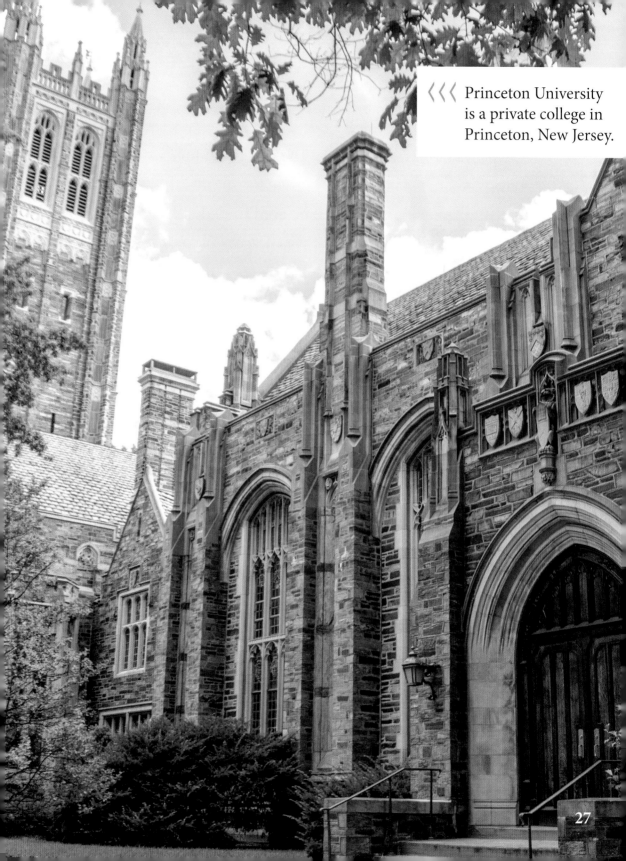

Princeton University is a private college in Princeton, New Jersey.

Kim will be 21 years old at the 2022 Winter Olympics. That's often the best age for many athletes. For Kim, it may be the end. The gold medalist has been snowboarding since she was 4 years old.

Kim has said she might retire after the 2022 Olympics. She wants to continue her studies and become a scientist. She has also talked about how hard the sport is on her body. One thing is for sure—Chloe Kim has a bright future, whatever she decides to do!

TIMELINE

2000 born on April 23 in Long Beach, California

2004 learned to snowboard with her father in California

2014 earned a silver medal in the superpipe competition at her first X Games

2016 won three X Games gold medals before the age of 16

2016 captured two gold medals at the Winter Junior Olympics in Norway

2016 became the first woman in snowboarding history to land back-to-back 1080-flips in competition and earned a perfect score of 100

2018 became the youngest female athlete to win an Olympic gold medal in a snow event

2019 suffered first major injury and breaks ankle at the U.S. Open in Vail, Colorado

2019 began studies at Princeton University

GLOSSARY

1080-DEGREE FLIP (1080 dih-GREE flip)—a trick where the snowboarder completes three full spins in the air before landing

COMPETITORS (kuhm-PE-tuh-tuhrz)—people who are trying to win in a sport or game

EMIGRATED (EM-i-greyt)—to leave one country and move to another one

HALF-PIPE (haf-pipe)—a ramp covered in snow curved at both ends and used to perform tricks

INTERNATIONAL (in-tur-NASH-uh-nuhl)—including more than one nation

SLOPE STYLE (slohp stahyl)—a snowboarding event that includes obstacles like rails and jumps added to the course

SOCIAL MEDIA (SOH-shuhl MEE-dee-uh)—forms of electronic communication used to share information, ideas, personal messages, and other content

SUPERPIPE (SOO-per-pipe)—a half-pipe but with higher walls and a larger flat surface in the middle

SWISS APLS (swis alps)—a mountain range in Europe

VIRAL (VYE-ruhl)—quickly and wide spread

READ MORE

Butler, Erin. *Extreme Snow and Ice Sports*. North Mankato, MN: Capstone Press, 2017.

Labrecque, Ellen. *Snowboarding*. North Mankato, MN: Cherry Lake Publishing, 2018.

McKinney, Donna. *STEM in Snowboarding*. Minneapolis: Abdo, 2017.

INTERNET SITES

Olympic Channel: Snowboarding
www.olympicchannel.com/en/sports/snowboarding

Sports Illustrated Kids: Snowboarding
www.sikids.com/2016/01/29/tips-learning-ski-and-snowboard-three-champs-mountain

World Snowboard Federation
www.worldsnowboardfederation.org

INDEX